BRIAN BOULDREY

The Sorrow of the Elves

Brian Bouldrey is the author of three novels: *The Genius of Desire, Love, The Magician* and *The Boom Economy*; three nonfiction books: *Honorable Bandit: A Walk Across Corsica, Monster: Adventures in American Machismo* and *The Autobiography Box* and editor of several anthologies. Brian teaches writing at Northwestern University.

Brian is North American Series Editor for Gemma Open Door.

GEMMA
Open Door

First published by GemmaMedia in 2011.

GemmaMedia
230 Commercial Street
Boston, MA 02109 USA

www.gemmamedia.com

Printed in the United States of America

15   14   13   12   11   1   2   3   4   5

978-1-934848-51-7

Library of Congress Cataloging-in-Publication Data

Bouldrey, Brian.
  The sorrow of the elves / Brian Bouldrey.
     p. cm. -- (Gemma open door)
  ISBN 978-1-934848-51-7
  1. Authors--Fiction. 2. Drug abuse--Fiction. 3. Psychological fiction.
I. Title.
  PS3552.O8314S67 2011
  813'.54--dc22
                              2010045820

Inspired by the Irish series of books designed for adult literacy, Gemma Open Door Foundation provides fresh stories, new ideas and essential resources for young people and adults as they embrace the power of reading and the written word.

GEMMA
Open Door

for Scott, Lynn, Cate, and Lily
gelato, gelato, gelato, gelato.

ONE

Here Comes the Sun King

First, all you can see is darkness. Then, with a blaze of blue fire, a face appears, like a sun in a black sky. It is our hero. His face is so bright in this flame, it makes the world behind him seem even darker than it was before he lit the stove.

You know what a hero is. A hero does brave deeds. In the old stories, the hero does not want things to change. The hero wants things to go back to the way things were, the way they were in the good old days. Back in the good old days, it was easy to know what the good old days were. These days, it is hard to tell what the good old days look like until they are long gone, gone to a place where we can not go any more. A place where heroes saw the dentist twice a year, bathed weekly, fed the dog every day, and never, ever swore.

These days, we do not always know what a hero looks like. Modest, they used to wear armor that covered all those muscles. They said nice things to ladies. These days, not only is it hard to see a hero for what he is, but it is hard to say what a lady is. You only use the word lady when a woman is a bad driver. "Lady, didn't you see that stop sign?" Or you use the word lady when she is a ... you know ... lady of the night. "Lady" is a four-letter word. We don't use the word "lady" sincerely, the way they used to. We say it with a bit of a smirk. Everybody, these days, has a smirk for a smile. Oh, for the old days, when ladies were ladies, when the hero was strong and never smirked or swore, when there was always beer in the fridge, when every day was a perfect magical summer day, and you had to brush flower petals off the dog, just to take him for a walk.

But there are still heroes, and there are still good people, and bad people, and magic, and my job is to tell you about a man who believed in that place that was before, and wants to get back to that place. He is the hero of this story. But he does not look like the old heroes. It is my job to point out the heroes, and the ladies, and the magic, and the journey the hero makes, the quest, which every hero must take on, if he is to be a hero.

Our hero is Walace Weiss. He is not big on armor or muscles. But you can tell that he is different because he chose to remove one of the l's from his name, "Wallace" to "Walace," in order to stand out from the rest of us. He may look like a normal person, but on the page, he is not normal.

Walace looks like a squat turkey, the sort that stands in the road just waiting for a car to hit him. It doesn't help that I present him here, for the first time, bending over a glowing blue gas ring with Cal. He looks even more like a fat bird as he tries not to burn his eyebrows as he takes an offered pipe from Cal, which may be short for California, or Caliban, or Calorie, depending on what Cal tells him from day to day.

"It is too hot," Cal tells Walace.

"The pipe, or the fire?" Walace does not usually draw on such pipes. He finds it bad for the lungs.

The pipe is not an ordinary pipe, made of corncob or walnut. It is a special pipe, made of clear, perfect glass. Glass is odd, you know. It is not a solid. It is always a liquid. If you have ever been to a very old church and looked at the stained glass pictures, you can see the glass sag into teardrops inside the leading. Cal's pipe sags like this. But that is probably because of the heat of the gas ring.

"Let it cool," says Walace. Cal does not want to let it cool. If he could, he would sit at the gas ring all day and draw on the pipe. In fact, he leans in again. Then Walace says, "Your baseball cap is on fire."

Cal's shoulders jerk, and he runs to and fro, saying that he is looking for a "fire distinguisher." You will see that Cal uses the wrong word at times. But that makes Walace happy. Cal is like a jester to Walace. Do not trust that Cal says the right thing all the time. Walace pulls him to the kitchen sink and turns on the spigot.

When Cal runs the cold water, it splashes like a brook over a dozen dirty plates and spoons and forks and pools with old food into half-empty cups. Neither of them has cleaned the kitchen in more than a week. It smells that way. There is a brief sizzle when the hat fire goes out. Walace says nothing.

Cal knows what he is thinking. "You got yourself a regular drug attic, don't you?"

Cal is also Walace's fix-it man. He fixes things around Walace's large house. He even fixes things that Walace did not know needed fixing. Cal is not a hero; if he were in one of the old tales, he would be the trickster guy, the naughty half-brother who might do something nice for you, or might do something nice for your enemy. He can work magic on an engine, or a broken stove, or a dead car battery. With a car battery, Cal can turn cold medicine into a potion that makes our hero feel young, strong, and brave. Our hero is still silent. Cal says, "You don't like me, do you?" Cal has said this often in the five weeks since he has moved into Walace's house with many bedrooms.

This time, after our hero turns off the stove and the kitchen is dark again, Walace says, "Of course I like you. You remind me of my Uncle Davis. I saw that when you had your face so close to the fire.

"Uncle Davis loved cigars. He had a house on a lake, and I would visit him when I was a kid. He would get up very early, before the sun, the way we are up before the sun now. He would light his first cigar off the fire on the stove, and I would see his face in that light. I would see it the way I see your face in the light now. Then he would go to the bathroom. He would sit on the toilet and smoke the whole cigar and let the ash drop into the bowl between his legs. By the time he came out of the bathroom, he had something to talk to me about. He liked me because I was a smart boy. He would have a math problem or a word game for me to solve. The day before he died, he told me that there were only six big words in the dictionary that had no vowels. One was syzygy. It was my job to find the other five words. Then he died."

"How did he die?" Cal asks, putting scotch tape on the burnt bill of his hat so that the cloth does not curl up. It has the mascot of the local college team on it—a bull.

"He did not see that the ashes from his cigar fell into his pubic hair and they caught on fire and he burned his house down."

Cal, who feels the effects of the pipe, laughs at this. "He burned his own genicals?"

But Walace Weiss is remembering that lost man, that lost house, that lost time. He says, "I never found those other words in the dictionary." But Walace believes that it was this quest that made him what he is today—a writer.

Walace Weiss is a famous writer of fantasy novels. He prefers the word romance to fantasy, but that makes people think of flowers and Fabio and girdles. It is Uncle Davis who made him a world-famous writer. Having Cal in the house comforts him, as if a bit of the old magic world were here, in this dirty kitchen.

As he walks away, Cal is saying, "Hey boss, what the hell is a sygazy?"

Walace used to know, but he doesn't any more: a syzygy is the lining up of three things in space: moons, planets, suns.

Even in the light before dawn, even in the shadow under the damaged cap, Walace can see Cal's eyelashes are gone, and that his brows have a plastic shine, as if he is wearing one of those nose-and-glasses that make people look like Groucho Marx. He places the pipe back in his mouth, the way Groucho did with his cigars.

Walace is glad he has not smoked too much from Cal's pipe, because although it makes him brave and strong, it also makes him feel ruthless. Smoking the drug from a pipe feels wasteful. Heroes do not like to waste things. Walace has his own way of using the little crystals that Cal makes for both of them, and Cal's pals who give him money for his magic potions.

Walace closes his bedroom door. He needs the light of a lamp to prepare, but it is too bright so he throws a shirt over the lampshade. From a dresser drawer, he pulls a pack of syringes. Cal calls them his darts. "Are you throwing darts?" he calls up the staircase.

Walace pulls the orange cap from the top. The orange cap shows that this needle is fresh, not used. He pours crystals onto a clean piece of paper, and rolls his good writing pen over all of it, crushing the crystals into powder. Then he slides the powder into the orange cap. When he pulls the plunger out of the long tube of the syringe it makes a popping sound. The sound excites Walace, because this is a romance, a romance of steel— the syringe is like a weapon. He uses the weapon to fight normal days, and the popping is the sound of taking the blade from its sheath. Uncle Davis would make that same sound by putting a finger in his mouth and pulling it out quickly. You know that sound.

He fills the thing with powder and water. When he is sure all the powder is dissolved, he uses a strong rubber band on his biceps, blots the inside crook of his elbow, and places the needle where he can feel it resist a bit, then give as the dart enters the river of his own blood.

I am telling you too much, perhaps. But you must see that for Walace Weiss, this moment is the whole story, a romance, a doorway into the magic worlds of his own novels. Soon, he will be like every character he has ever invented: hero, dragon, maiden trapped by dragon, a lawless wizard trickster like Cal, women with dark powers, fisher kings with wounds that never heal, and the creatures he is most famous for writing about, the immortal elves.

So let me tell you a little more, and then I promise I will not speak these dark words again. He draws back a little on the plunger to make sure he is in the vein. There is a report of red, a red that looks like smoke in the clear fluid. Then, with a sure swift push, the red report, the clear fluid, all of it is no longer in the needle, but slammed deep into his body. In three quick moves, he tosses the needle aside, pulls off the rubber band, and presses the swab once again to his skin. Yes, Cal, Walace has thrown a dart.

TWO

New Life

And then what happened? Youth, power, bravery, yes. But first, all of his long muscles, the ones in his arms and legs, they flex in his body. A real pick-me-up. But the ones that dilate, around the heart, the tiny ones in the pupils of his eye, his very sphincter, these all dilate, for what are these but ring-shaped bundles of long muscles, pulling tight. How funny, that muscles can flex to relax. "The heart dilates," Walace says out loud as the buzzing comes to his ear and a cough comes from his lungs, taking on the extra cargo in his blood stream. But though it his heart he last thinks of for a while, it is his eyes that jiggle in his skull, as if somebody has pulled back the shades too quickly. He lies back on his bed and lets the rush rush. He wishes he had the brains or power to take his clothes off.

Cal stands at the foot of the stairs. Who knows how long he has stood there. Who knows how long Walace Weiss has dilated. Hours. Days. Years.

"Uh-oh," says Cal, which makes Walace get off the bed, "Our professor has gone down the habit hole!"

"Stop calling me professor," says Walace, who does not need to teach at the college any more. He trundles down the stairs without falling. "And no, I haven't."

But the truth is, Walace is glad that Cal's ball cap had burned before he slammed, because he might not have said, "Your cap is on fire" now. Not because he is mean, not really. It is just that after Walace's heart opens, he does not go down any rabbit hole. He is always here, here where he is, except that his power seems to have been placed at the top of a tower, captive, like one of the elf maidens from his novels. In fact, this is the plot of his second novel, The Pleasure of the Elves, which we all have read, even Cal, who praised it for having some colorful pigments of the imagination.

From the tower of his body, eyes all pupil, Walace can see everything.

He can see when Cal's baseball cap is on fire, but now, for some reason, he would be unable to say, "Your cap is on fire." His dilated mind wants him to say such things, but some other person or army inside him, a knight dressed in black, or a dark lady with spells, keeps his mouth from speaking. He can only see, not do.

And he can see even more than what is there. He feels so creative, he could write ten books, if he could just find his good writing pen. That is his own quest as a hero—to find a way to break out of this tower, find a pen, and write a new story for the first time in twelve years.

Perhaps, he thinks, being in the kitchen will feel like coming down from the tower. Cal is calling him. That helps. But the moment he gets to the kitchen, Cal walks past him and heads upstairs. "Where are you going?" Walace asks. But he knows. Cal is going to the drug attic. In a room over the garage, Cal has set up his magic engine, the great lab where household things turn into potions.

"I have some clients coming today," says Cal. "And I've got work to do."

"Have you been able to fix my computer yet?" asked Walace, who sometimes sees his broken computer as the only thing that stops the new novel from getting done.

Cal shakes his head. "Rome wasn't burned in a day." Walace would not bother Cal with this, except it was

Cal, on his first day living here, who removed nearly every program on that computer, for fear of spies in the apps and cams, until it was nearly nothing but a lit screen and an off switch. Even then, Cal asked that Walace keep the screen covered with a heavy blanket. He'd fix it up good. It was on his to-do list. Until then, Walace could write his novel on notepads, like they did in the Days of Shivery.

It has been more than a month since Cal moved in. Cal's girlfriend, Wendy, who reads all of Walace's books, had thrown Cal out. Cal was sorry about that. He hoped Wendy might keep him in line, but she told Cal that she was not his mommy. Also, Cal did not like to be pinned down to just one girl.

Also, he had started a pretty bad fire in Wendy's tool shed. She had made it into a little office where she could write poems. When Cal's lab blast destroyed all of her verse and also sucked all the air from the windowless shed and choked her old cat, poor Syd, to death, that was the end of their true love. When Walace, her hero, took Cal in, she was a little surprised. But just a little. "Frankly, it explains a lot," she had said, oddly, to Walace when he came to pick up Cal in his dented Maserati.

Cal's lab—pretty much everything he owned—had also been lost in that fire. Walace invited him to stay in his house, a mansion he had built for himself from the profits of his three bestselling novels and the movie rights to the first, *The Delight of the Elves*. The mansion was called Summerheim, after the elf nation in his books. It was closed in by a high fence with elvish script telling all who pass by of something important to elves. Wendy knew a little elvish, for her elf poems. "Welcome to my McBrothel," she believes it says, "Boy whores take the room over the garage." That was where Walace has put Cal.

But you and I know that Cal is not a whore, and Walace has always liked girls, though, without his love darts he finds them hard to talk to. He would be hurt to hear Wendy speak this way of Cal, of his home, and of his elves. He thinks Wendy is pretty. And she writes poems in elvish. There was a time when Wendy was one of Walace's biggest fans.

Walace has all the tools from the fix-it guy who lived here before Cal, over the garage. Cal is the latest in a long line of fix-it guys. At the moment, Walace is sorry he has forgotten some of their names, but they come and go so quickly. Sometimes they don't take care of themselves and they have to go to the hospital. Sometimes they walk out the front door and do not come back. One even got into Walace's bright red Maserati, and that was that. It turned up along the side of a road two states away, two months later. Not that Walace was using it. His own driver's license has expired, as has the insurance. He was going to get to that.

He does not tell people this, but Walace is sad about all the wizards he'd hosted before Cal—all the Cals of yore. People do not know this, but his last novel, what people are wrong to call the last book of his trilogy, the book called *The Desire of the Elves*, was about all the old Cals. If you recall, Brangane the Elf King rode into battle on his noble jackrabbit after having one too many thimbles of mead and got himself hurt in the thigh by a troll-sword. Although the elf-maidens came to his bedroom each day and cleaned the sore, even though the wizard Amfeto brought new cures to his highness, the gash never healed. Only the she-elf princess Lancelotte saved him after she had been freed from her tower prison by Werther, the half-elf, the saddest knight in Summerheim. Lancelotte denied her sad champion, Werther, in order to come to the Elf King's bed and offer herself to Brangane.

First, she poured from a jug another thimble of mead for her king, who rested on a couch of silk pillows. She kneeled before him and loosened the rabbit-hair lace of her elf vest. She took the king's own hand and placed it beneath that vest. Beneath the vest, there was no blouse, no girdle—just elf-maid skin, fair and pink and immortal

Outside, Lancelotte could hear the hitched-up jackrabbits fuss in the corral, and was that Werther sighing, weeping a little into his own fisted hand? No matter—Summerheim needed her more than Werther. She let the king open her elf vest, and hold one of her elfin breasts. The king's hand did not expose but protect, the way she-elf warriors' armor both protected and described the friendly skin beneath. Lancelotte's sighs of sweet content out-sighed Werther's sighs of lonesome sorrow. And when she looked to Brangane's elf-loins, she saw that his gash was slowly closing.

The king took his scepter into his hands for the first time in an age. As she gave herself fully to her king and country, she allowed herself to hear a single jackrabbit saddled, mounted, spurred, and encouraged by a brave, sad warrior. But she knew Werther, however sad, would be riding through a never-ending summer of falling peony petals, where mead ran in waterfalls and no one ever cursed. Only then did the open sore stop weeping, and Summerheim itself, without sun or sky for a decade, become restored to its former glory.

Cal has powers of his own, Walace figures. Cal seems to always tell when Walace is thinking about his novels. He is always thinking about his novels, really, always looking for scraps of paper to write down ideas for his novels. The kitchen table is covered with notes. Some can even be read. "Syd is a free bird." Some even make sense. "The male nightingale is the one that sings."

Lately, Walace got a sort of promise from his editor, and he even thinks about giving himself a deadline. "I should work on my novel today," he says to Cal. "I wish I had my computer."

"You should write them on notepads. The great writers write on notepads. I know how you feel about computers," Cal says.

Walace hates computers. They are an evil he must live with.

Cal hands him three long legal pads, goldenrod yellow. He hands him three magic markers, which are not pens. Cal always jokes that Walace likes Sharpies. "You should go!" Cal pushes. "I will take care of things here! Go write your book!" Cal tells him that he will call on his cell phone when all the dealing has been conducted and everything is honky-tonky.

It isn't until Walace is walking out of the gates of his own Summerheim that he realizes he has not charged the cell phone for days. It is as dead as a doornail. Is it his imagination, or can he hear the flint and steel click of the kitchen stove, even here on the street? When he is high, he often has super-hearing. Who needs a cell phone, when you have the keen elf-ears of a hero?

THREE

Patience is a Virtue

When Walace Weiss has romanced the steel like this, it is as if he has become the potion he has placed in himself. As if he has taken two clamps and fixed the ends to the car battery sitting in Cal's tower room over the garage, and the other ends to himself, and revved the engine. He would write at least five chapters now, if he could only find a pen.

It makes him feel as bold as the knights of old, as if he could sweep into any disco and scoop the prettiest dancer in the room and take her back to his kingdom. As soon, of course, as Cal allows him to come back to Summerheim, which is his kingdom and his home. It is as if all the joy is suddenly squeezed from the joy glands in his body all at once. Just walking here on the sidewalk is like riding a roller coaster. When Walace Weiss is amped like this, he is not afraid of anything: girls, students, former fans. Not even his editor.

Cate, his editor, has been as patient as a maid trapped in a tower guarded by a dragon. She does not call him for his books, at least not any more. She simply waits until he comes to her. And when he finally does come to her, every two years or so, she is always hopeful.

Cate and Walace have known each

other for years. He likes to think that there was a chance of love between them, but they were both wise and remained friends. She is an excellent editor, one of his most careful readers. They have seen each other through books and lovers and cigarettes and births and deaths and victories and defeats. Walace recalls the first cigarette he had ever seen Cate smoke. He remembers the day he thanked her for all her help with *The Delight of the Elves* by giving her a case of cigarettes. This was twelve years ago.

"You are a love," she said, ripping open a carton and lighting a cigarette there in her office, even if it was against the law. This was, after all, a celebration.

"Make those last," Walace had chided, "they are not good for you."

"Are you kidding?" Cate said, the cigarette bobbing on each word at the side of her mouth, "Cigarettes keep me healthy!" She explained the way the smoke entered her lungs and spread through her bloodstream, a tarry weapon against all the diseases that threatened her body. No germ could survive the daily smoke bombs with which she attacked her body's foes. "I don't even get the common cold," she boasted.

Walace had been inspired by her.

He remembers the day he brought a case to celebrate the blockbuster movie based on his novel, the day he published *The Pleasure of the Elves,* and *The Desire of the Elves.* How she had taken his large box with a cry of joy. And he remembers the last time he saw her, just a month ago, and tried to smooth over any hard feelings between them. After all, he promised her, over the years, six other elf novels. Gave her the first chapters, and one time the first section, of four of them.

When he came in with that first page of *The Sorrow of the Elves* sitting on top of a crate of cigarettes, she had said, "You have to get that out of my office right now, Walace. You're only making it difficult."

He was sure she meant the first page of the novel. But she rolled up her sleeve and showed him a nicotine patch. It thrilled Walace to see lady skin, and it relieved him to know that it was the cigarettes she did not want. She coughed.

"Common cold?" he joshed.

"Emphysema," she said. Walace thought of Uncle Davis then, too. He had had emphysema, but it didn't stop him from smoking! But Uncle Davis never saw Walace become the great writer. He never saw how he had set his nephew on the road to being the hero he was today.

Walace needs to find the other word with no vowels. Syzygy, he thought. He remembers a thing he should not have forgotten: a syzygy is a lineup of three astral bodies. He was pleased to remember like that. That is the tough thing for elves: they live forever, and have to remember everything. The elves would have known what a syzygy was. And remembered. The elves would have known the other words that did not need vowels.

"And how is your health?" Cate said, just to remind him that he was standing in her office with a crate of cigarettes. "You've lost some weight."

Was that praise? She had gained some weight, but that's what happens when you quit smoking. "You are a strong woman," Walace said. "Everywhere you go, people smoke cigarettes. Every store has cigarettes. You can bum a cigarette off a stranger. I don't think I could quit cigarettes."

Cate smiled. "They say that the people who have the hardest time quitting are smart people, famous people, and pretty people."

What can Walace Weiss do, then?

He said, "I've been working on a new novel. *The Sorrow of the Elves.*" He came wanting to discuss a contract. Years ago, he fired his agent after a fight. He prefers handling money matters himself now. But Cate did not give him a contract. Instead, she went to a closet where she hung her coat and hid her filing cabinet. She showed him four poster-sized blow-ups of his novel jackets, mock-up covers taken to sales meetings to sell his books. They were mounted on foam core. They were lovely, paintings of the elves and jackrabbits of his novels. They had titles like *"The Shunning of the Elves,"*

"The Cup Bearer of the Elves," and *"The Homefires of the Elves."* Don't strain yourself trying to remember—these books do not exist.

"I will make a deal with you," Cate said. Usually this is when she would light up another cigarette. Instead, she rubbed her little nicotine patch nervously. "I will write you a contract if you give me two hundred pages of *The Sorrow of the Elves.*"

Walace's eyes grew big behind the thick lenses of his glasses. For a moment, he did not look like a turkey. He looked like a koala. "No problem!" Walace had said. This time, he knew exactly how the story would go.

She saw him to the door, and rubbed his back with warm care. "And

Walace," she said gently. "You should quit."

"Writing?" he said. "It's the only thing I can do."

If somebody could smile and frown at the same time, then that is what Cate did. This is what the dark lady of his novels did, the ones who had power, power they hid until it was needed.

That day, he carried the crate of cigarettes home and gave them to Cal as a housewarming present, a party for the looming success of *The Sorrow of the Elves*.

FOUR

The Sorrow of the Elves

And who does not know the noble origins of Werther the half-elf, and his long life of regret? Even if you had never read a word of Walace Weiss' three great books, the world has seen the dazzling last scene of the movie made from *The Delight of the Elves*. In that scene his mother, the guide of war-jackrabbits, mere hours after giving birth to her only son in the bunny-down safety of her own steed's nest, leaves Werther to be raised by rabbits. And that is how she led the last troop of rabbits and elves against the ravens and stone trolls. How she

hid her breast under a walnut shield.
How she concealed her golden hair
beneath a helmet made from an acorn
top. How even her name was a mask:
Syd. How, on a normal patrol just
hours before the final battle, she had
been mortally wounded, so young,
by a flying wedge of ravens. How she
ordered her page, in her dying breath,
to lash her body upright on her
jackrabbit, the noble Boris, to hide
her death. And how she spurred Boris
out onto the battle field to the army's
cry, "Elf Syd! Elf Syd! Elf Syd!"

How Boris was not afraid to carry
Werther's mother's corpse into the
fight and die a noble death. How all
the elves followed that brave body
and bunny and won the battle for

Summerheim. How the Morning Goddess blessed the elves, in honor of Syd's bravery, by giving the rest of the elves endless life.

Why would Werther not be proud of a mother like that? Her death had meant life for all her kin. What is a little bird going to do if he sees Werther's pouting lower lip? Toughen up, Werther! You're an elf warrior!

Walace Weiss plans to show all the woes of Werther in his new book, *The Sorrow of the Elves*. As he walks down the street to the college where, years ago, he taught writing, he taps his head as if to say, "Not to worry. It's all right up here." As he does this, other people on the sidewalk step away, perhaps afraid his elbow will hit them as he swings it up, tapping, then down, then up, tapping, then down, and so forth.

This is the first page, the one he wanted to show Cate last month:

What no one knows but suffering Werther is the terrible fate of Werther's father, Tithon. Did not the early death of Syd define the very problem of elf immortality? How can the immortal fade away? What does it really mean to live forever? No one is crazy about dying, but is the other fate, life without ending, such a great idea?

Tithon knew. He knew before the elves. Tithon was not an elf, but a wandering sylph, a gypsy sylph. He loved Syd against her family's wishes. And after Syd's death, the lack of love from his in-laws led to great misery. For he was the first to get the Morning Goddess's blessing. In honor of his wife's brave deeds, the gods promised Tithon, first, that he had seen enough of death. Tithon was handsome (for a sylph,) like his son. The Morning Goddess liked that. Tithon, in his loneliness, became the Morning Goddess's lover.

But the sisters of Syd did not like this. The sisters of Syd believed that it was Tithon's duty to grieve out his life for his dead wife, and to raise his sad son, rather than have him suckle at the teat of jackrabbits. Syd's sisters, who were earth elves, conjured magic of their own. Tithon would have endless life. But he would not have endless youth.

Werther watched his father grow older and older: gray-haired, white-haired, no-haired, his bones like tent stakes holding up the frail canopy of his skin, skin that could be ripped by a rose thorn. His father went to the Morning Goddess each day and begged for an end to this, but we all know that what the gods give, the gods cannot take away.

There goes Werther, on his way to the elf pub, head low over his rabbit-steed, lost in the sadness of his own life: the son of a mother given youth without immortality, and a father given immortality without youth. Werther, sad Werther, neither elf nor sylph, unbound by any nation, but bound by *family duty to grieve forever, until the dying of Summerheim itself!*

See Werther belly up to the elf bar and order his first thimble of mead! See him dilute the potent draught with his own tears! Another round, Barkeep Elf! For this potion will never be potent enough!

And then Walace plans to tell the story of Werther's attempts to please the Elf King and defend Summerheim, and live without desire for the Elf King's wife, the fair Lancelotte. And he would tell of the very bad betrayal of the Elf King and Summerheim as Werther took Lancelotte in a fairy ring of toadstools that had a strange magic, in which all of Summerheim could hear their lovemaking, how the old wound in the Elf King's leg opened again, and the king and

Werther would have to fight against each other, in order to save or destroy Elfdom.

Walace taps his head again: it is all right up here. He steps through the door of the campus library, still tapping. A little snatch of bold music, invented by his dilated heart, trumpets through his lips. People step aside, making way for our hero.

FIVE

A Hero's Welcome

"Aren't all jackrabbits boys? How can Werther suckle at the teat of a jackrabbit when all jackrabbits are boys? Sounds pretty gay to me."
—signed, TerribleTina@yahoo.co.uk

"What the hell is a sylph?"
—signed, CalamityCon@hotmail.com

The fans. That damn internet. The stupid ungrateful fans. Walace Weiss has arrived at the college library, hoping to find his carrel empty, even though it has been almost six years since the school employed him. After all, for three years before that he rarely went to the carrel and nobody touched it, though it could have used some dusting. But the college honors Professor Weiss's workplace as if it were the tomb of a king.

Since the last time he has been to this library, there have been some changes. The room that had once featured books written by college teachers is now filled with computers. In the dim room, students sit staring in the glow of a hundred screens, as if they are members of a submarine crew peering into blipping radar screens, searching for battleships to sink. Battleships like the S.S. Summerheim, captained by our hero, Walace Weiss.

Walace would have walked right past the torpedo launchers. But he is trying to remember what nook or cranny they had placed his little office in (Floor 3? Floor 5? South Tower? West Tower?) Then he remembers that a month ago he had posted the opening paragraph of *The Sorrow of the Elves* on his fansite, *www. sensualelves.com,* and it would be easy enough to print out the page, take it to his study, and go on with his work without starting over. When he steers to the site, he finds it has been defaced by any number of so-called fans like Terrible Tina and Calamity Con. It is as if his entire career has been attacked by a gang of thugs. Mobbed, is the word they are using these days.

Walace Weiss has no use for words they are using these days. Walace wants only things that endure. If the elves could live without the internet, then so can he. He doesn't need cars, or credit cards, or cell phones, or fans.

"Aren't elves as tall as us? Orlando Bloom would squash a jackrabbit."
—signed Legolas96@badboy.com

"The elves have got it wrong. The elves don't want anything to change, because they don't want to have to remember anything, or miss anybody who dies or greet somebody new. That's just unhealthy."
—signed PeterPansWendy@aol.com

"Dear 'fans,'"
Walace Weiss's fingers clatter across the keyboard, another thing that will not endure. He has spilled any number of things into any number

of keyboards, and knows about the fleeting life of keyboards. His fingers hit harder at the letters the deeper into his message he goes. His heart is not dilating right now.

> "Dear 'fans,'
> Jackrabbits are not male rabbits. Jackrabbits are actually hares, not rabbits. Hares are larger than rabbits, and they have taller hind legs and longer ears. Jackrabbits were named for their ears, which is why people first called them 'jackass rabbits.' Does your mother refer to you, too, as a jackass rabbit? She ought to.
> —Sincerely, WW"

There are more errors than I have shown here, but it is clear enough. The fans have stopped reading, stopped believing in anything that endures, and only watch Hollywood versions of things. They think elves are movie stars or spacemen.

It may come as a surprise to readers that long ago, Walace Weiss had a wife. Long before even his first story about the elves, the story not put in any book, but called "The Nation of the Elves," the story in which he showed the long trip the elves made in order to find Summerheim. Walace's wife, Laura-Lynn, liked things that made her five senses feel good. She liked good food, good booze, good beds, and good sex in good beds. She was the one who pushed him to invent elf sex, the thing he was most famous for in fantasy. Sex, after all, endured. This was the test for all of his writing, and it was all her idea: Would the elves drink beer? Would the elves have satin sheets? These were things that have lasted since the Age of Elves.

What did not last was their marriage. It was twelve years ago, a night just after he had slammed. He sat looking at the screen door in the old house, the house before Summerheim was built, and saw a dying butterfly slowly folding and unfolding its wings. He stood watching it for hours, probably, as if he were a child looking into a View-Master at a 3-D pattern. The high, greedy artist in him was waiting for the pattern on the butterfly's wings to change. Instead, it just died. By the time he realized the butterfly was dead, his wife had packed up and left him, without even a note.

And over those twelve years, both waiting for Laura-Lynn to return and building his awful anger toward her, he began to think like an elf, to understand the elves. For the elves withdrew from the world of men, shrank in size so they could not be seen by men or be mistaken for Orlando Fucking Bloom, because men, well, men died. Or their love for each other died. Love ought to last. People ought to last. Instead, they disappeared, and hurt. Walace Weiss built his iron fence.

The elvish script along the pickets did not say anything about boy whores. Instead, it read, "We elves do not suffer death from old age or disease, but we can be killed by our weariness of the world and our own grief." This was a lot of pricey wrought iron. And the fence had to be a lot longer than Walace had planned. He had to take care of the lawn within the area confined by that long fence. Lately, it had become an untended weedy field. Somebody on his fan page had taken a picture of himself in front of his fence and written, "Me Outside the Haunted McMansion." He would call a landscaper tomorrow, if he thought of it, and if he could recharge his phone.

Walace wonders whether he can remove that photo from the web. After all, it is a site about him. He turns to the frat boy sitting next to him. Probably here for summer school because he is drinking too much at frat house parties, flunking out. "Do you know how to remove something from a website?" The boy has nearly stepped away twice in the last few minutes, and Walace agrees that it might be the fact that Walace is sweating. He has taken to wearing long-sleeved shirts to hide the bruised places along his arms where the darts go in wrong, and in the heat of the summer and the panicked fury that swelled through him when he read TerribleTina's idiotic question, he is a mask of sweat. The boy stands up. He says, "Dude, the internet is, like, forever." He walks away.

Such a risky, fair-weather friend is the internet. Full of temptation. Walace bets he could find the other words that require no vowels right now, right here, but the elves know that it is the hunt, not the kill, that keeps a hero going. Walace thought of a nice plot line for his novel: Werther is also sad because his nightingale, Syzygy, a bird his elf aunts told him contained the soul and song of his dead mother, had escaped its golden cage and flown away, perhaps out of Summerheim itself.

Walace expects his heart to dilate a little with that thought. Instead, he hits his hip against a table, and it hurts a lot. So his heart does not open but shrinks a little bit. Soon it will be time to bump up. As if the elf gods themselves were blessing his decision, he sees a poster on the wall with a dartboard and a single dart at the very center. "Bull's eye!" it says in bold script. But there are a lot of pictures of darts and bull's eyes on campus. The team mascot is a bull.

And that is why he carries two eyeglass cases, one for his glasses, for he is famously farsighted. The ungrateful fans call him "coke-bottle four-eyes with patches on his sport coat." The sport coat has deep pockets, one for his glasses, one for his rig.

He takes a book off the library shelf, making a flat place where he can set up his rig. I promised earlier that I would not describe these strange acts again, but I ask you, what hero does not draw his power from outside himself? Popeye with his spinach? Thor with his hammer? Underdog with his secret energy pill? Ultraman with whatever that thing is?

Walace does it selflessly. He does it for you. It once gave him the power to stay up all night to write the stories we needed. Now he uses it to give him the power to face ungrateful fans and angry editors. It gives him the power to roam the world seeking a quiet place to do his work. It makes him feel so creative, he could write two hundred pages if he could just find his good writing pen.

Walace steps out of a restroom the way Superman steps out of a phone booth. And yes, Cal, the professor has thrown another dart.

SIX

A Hero's Quest

"Hello, Doctor Weiss!" Here is a cheerful face, a human face that has turned away from the cold blue deep-sea screens. She recognizes him, and she is smiling.

"Hello, young lady," he says, for his heart has dilated again, and she is young, but not so young that she does not have some power of her own in this great maze of knowledge. She is waiting for something, something from the hero—our hero—her hero.

"You don't remember me, do you, Doctor Weiss?"

An old student. Of course, he cannot be expected to know every student from his past. A hero meets many admiring peasants in his adventures. How many times have they come to his bookstore signings and nearly shamed him by asking for an inscription. "And how do you spell that again?" he will ask, when they do not volunteer their name right away.

"B-I-L-L," one said, such a sourpuss.

The young happy librarian says, "I was in your Reading and Writing Children's Stories class many years ago. Gosh, when was that? Around the time of that John Wayne Bobbitt mess."

What an odd marker of time! But truly, world events, which do not endure, baffle our hero. He has heard that there was a flood in New Orleans. He has heard that there are wars in the Middle East. He has no time for the details. A hero has work to do here, always here and now.

As if to jog his slammed memory, she tells him about the workshop at the end of the course, in which each student had to write his own children's story. "My story began, 'Brangane the elf got off his jackrabbit, hitched it to a post, entered the elf bar, and ordered his first thimble of mead.' Does that sound familiar?"

Of course it sounds familiar. Clearly the girl has copied the work he has done in the last few months. Ten years ago. Isn't that one of the funny things about immortality? Time runs in funny ways. This is what Walace is thinking, and does not nod to the girl. She goes on. "There was this girl, kinda daffy. Brandelyn. We all remember because you wrote on each of our stories, 'Note during workshop: do not do what Brandelyn is telling you to do to fix your story.' You were very careful, Dr. Weiss. We all thought she was silly, but you never said she was silly in class, so we didn't know what you thought until we came to my story."

And then Walace does recall. It was on a day when he was first dilating his heart, and he was not quite in control of it. He recalled that this girl Brandelyn had said in class, "I would like to know sooner in the story that I am reading a fantasy." And Walace had leaned forward, pounded the table with his fist, and shouted, "For Summerheim's sake, Brandelyn. He just got off his jackrabbit. What more do you need?" The entire class had burst out laughing. Except for Brandelyn. She had burst into tears.

"That was a great class," the librarian says.

"I'm glad," says Walace. But now that he has a lady-champion, he must finish his quest with her help. "My dear, I'm here to see if I might get a new key to my old office. I seem to have lost mine."

Her smile grows firm—not fake, not blank, but the smile of the resolved.

"I'm pretty sure your old carrel was cleared out, Dr. Weiss. I was the one who told them you would come back for it. And here you are!" He looks past her, to see if somebody else can help him. But she is to be his champion. "Let me see whether we can find the box with all your things. Maybe I can help you set everything up again. I could be your research helper!"

Walace likes this idea. "You have had training?"

She nods as she walks over to a board with hooks and keys and numbers, as if she runs a little hotel. "Did you know that I am writing my paper on Harry Potter?"

Harry Potter. Here we go again. That crap. Every character, every scene, every theme, every battle, stolen from the classics. It will never endure. The author a thief. Making all the people of the world one nation of babies.

Walace doesn't know it, but he just said that aloud. He might realize this if he were looking at his former student, who has stopped looking for his key, or a key, or anything. Somewhere along the way, she has also lost her smile. Walace doesn't see this, and he does not see that she leaves her post for nearly five minutes. Time moves in an odd fast-slow-slow-fast way, as if it were a knotted rope being pulled around a large cleat, slipping and sticking. When she returns, she is with a guard. He is holding a box.

"Professor Weiss?" he says. "These

are your books. We are happy you've come to get them. Please take them with you as you leave now, because we will throw them away if you don't." The girl stands behind him. She says no more. Perhaps there was even more he did not know he said out loud. But it is clear that it is time for him to leave.

Without looking into the box, he leaves it by a big donation bin just outside the library. If he were only to look back, he would see that the librarian is crying. But for whom?

Never mind. This was a perfect day to go walking, a new summer day, one of the first hot ones. Wearing the long-sleeved shirt is foolish, wearing the old deep-pocket sport coat silly. But there

is a delight—a delight of the elves!—
to walk past cinderblock college town
bars and smell the air inside them,
colder, with a scent of stale beer,
cigarette butts, broken dreams.

He knows some of these bars, but
now that he throws darts, he doesn't
drink anymore. He wrote nearly all
of *The Delight of the Elves* when just
an undergraduate on student funds.
He could nurse a pint for hours while
describing the difference between
earth elves and wind elves and fire
elves. "We only allow fire elves in here,
bucko," Dugan, the bartender of The
Home Fires, had said when Walace
explained why he spent so much time
scribbling on pads of paper. After
that, Dugan always left him alone, but

told the other patrons of the strange dreams of our misunderstood hero. Walace gave Dugan one of the first copies of his first book when it came out, as if to say "Thanks" and "I told you so" at the same time.

After that, Dugan always gave him his first beer on the house. Then came the day when Dugan stopped serving him. Walace wonders now whether Dugan is still tending bar at The Home Fires. It might be a good place to work on *The Sorrow of the Elves*. He steps in, for the door is open, and the jukebox is playing something sad. Not much has changed except that the pinball machine has been replaced by a dartboard, and the cat in the window is now black, instead of orange. It's early for bars, and nobody serves or drinks. Walace has the bar to himself. He sits down in his old, old booth. It is like old, old times. The Home Fires— some things endure.

"Out you go, Doctor Elf," says Dugan, who, if anything, has gotten more flesh and more tattoos to put on the flesh over the years. "I cut you off, remember?"

Our hero leaves, not because he is afraid of his challenger, but because somewhere between the library and here, he has lost his writing pads. And wallet. Walace feels tragic, like his elves, for yes, he should have remembered. This is, after all, the true sorrow of the elves—they live so long that their greatest sin, their greatest wound, their greatest terror, is forgetting. Walace dreams, briefly, of the day he publishes *The Sorrow of the Elves* and gives one of the first copies to Dugan, another "Thanks" mixed with another "I told you so." It is the few mortal men like Dugan with whom the elves will spend time, because they know how to remember the main things.

Otherwise, Walace has written, the elves avoid humans, for they come and go so quickly in Summerheim, and the grief of elves lasts for years, a time longer than the lives of men themselves. Do not even ask me about the courtship of elves. Believe me, ladies, coyness is no crime in Summerheim.

By now, Walace is excited about his

new novel and all the things that are happening that would work so well in the story—not just Dugan, but our hero's journey and setbacks here and now, on the sidewalk, how he, like Werther, is shunned, misunderstood, a victim of bad timing.

There is that diner a little further up from The Home Fires, another place he wrote for a few weeks, until the terrible incident with the American Express bill wallet ("Why can't you take my American Express card? The bill is in a wallet that was given to you by American Express! I refuse to pay." And so forth.) There is the little park where he drew the maps of Summerheim, but the moms on the playground had mistrusted him so near their kids, staring and drawing, staring and drawing. A hero is alone, and a man alone is a man who lives a life of danger.

It shocks Walace as much as it shocks us to find him standing in front of Wendy's house, Cal's old house. He wonders whether Wendy has rebuilt her writing shed. In a splendid series of near-connected thoughts, he wonders whether he might rent the writing shed from her for a few hours each day. That is why, before we even know it, he has rung her doorbell and offered to pay her two hundred dollars a week if she will let him work in the shed each day before noon.

"Why," she says, "so I can replace one tweaker burning down my life with another?" She speaks to him through the screen door. He understands—it is summertime, and it is buggy.

Walace hates the word "tweaker." It is a word invented, no doubt, on the internet. Words have power, and must be clear. He does not like slang. Slang words are flabby words. A word must stay unspoken to keep its power, or it must be well-spoken. One day, soon after he moved in, Cal made the terrible mistake of calling it "crank."

"Crank?" pressed Walace, pretending not to know what Cal was talking about. Usually, Walace didn't really know what Cal was talking about, anyway. "Crank is something that starts an old car. Crank is somebody who believes in Bigfoot."

Cal was cranking up on his pipe and not in much of a mood for a grammar lesson. "Well, what do you call it, Professor?"

"Crystal methamphetamine," Walace said, clearly and bravely. "I believe you should be able to correctly spell anything you're going to put into your body." Which may be why he enraged all his fans from Europe after telling a reporter for sensualelves.com that he did not like French food.

Cal laughed at that. "If I had to spell everything that went into my body, boss, I would have starved to death years ago. And I don't plan on starving to death."

"How do you plan to die?" Walace had asked, because his life was with the elves, who did not understand death. Cal was a good human who may not have a good memory, but had a good feeling for what he was: flawed and mortal.

Cal said, "I think you grow a little pottied plant in yourself that is your death, and you tend it like it was a rose for the girl you love. Except my plant is not pot or potties. My plant is crank." Cal said it clearly and bravely, too, in his different way. "I plan to flame out in a great big crank-tastrophee." And then he blew smoke out of his lungs so thick, it was as if he were fading in some sort of opera stagecraft. Walace was almost stunned to see him still standing there after the smoke had cleared.

Now, Wendy seems stunned herself, because Walace is still standing on her stoop, lost in this memory. Memories find a thousand ways to slow our hero down. He realizes that she is waiting for him to say something, so he says, "I am not like Cal."

"No," she smiles, "No you are not. If there is one thing I've learned, it's that every tweaker is like a snowflake."

Even in this state, Walace can see that this chat is almost over. "I wouldn't be... tweaking in your shed. I would be writing *The Sorrow of the Elves*."

What is this tweaking they are speaking of? It is the thing that happens to Walace when he has not slept for days, when his brain is so tired it can get stopped by a simple thing— the loss of his best writing pen—and he cannot go on with what he wanted to do. When our hero has been tweaking for more than two days without rest, he notices that he becomes more aware. His skin is more sensitive, his senses are magnified, and he feels all the feelings others are feeling. This is a great power for a writer, who must describe the feelings of all those characters inside himself. Now, he sees at least a dozen feelings bubble up into Wendy's face, including hope, fear, doubt, forgiveness, resolve, wonder, and resolve again. To name a few. Only Walace, dilated, could see all this in the split second before she answers, "Why don't you kick Fonzie out of the room over the garage? That would be a great place to write your book."

He does not want to explain to her why he cannot be in his own home, let alone in Cal's drug attic. He asks her if she is still writing elvish poems—this used to be his best pickup line at The Home Fires. Or another version, when he was less of a hero and more of a cynic: He had picked up Laura-Lynn, almost twenty years ago, at a science fiction meeting when he was signing his book for her. He said, as he had said at least a hundred times before, "Why did you stop writing elvish poetry?"

"I've got to go, Walace. Good luck with your sad elf problem." And Wendy closes the inside door, which must be a great sacrifice, airflow-wise, since it is such a hot day.

Walace takes the stoop steps two at a time. He is at that place in a slam where his oomph and his high are still running smoothly. Not too many visions or mood swings yet. He should drink some water now. He always forgets to drink water, and he knows he should drink lots of water, because it's getting to be a hot day. He's two blocks away from his first house, the house he shared with Laura-Lynn. The house with the unchanging butterfly (the things Walace can remember could fill a book!). Perhaps she's back there. It was never sold. He didn't need to sell it to build Summerheim. It would be nice to see the old place again. It would be nice to see Laura-

Lynn again. They have both moved on, that is true, but Walace is a hero. A hero never salts the earth. A hero cleanses the earth.

But when he gets to the old house, the house that does not have a name like Summerheim, and, he consoles himself, therefore has no power, it is still empty. At least for the moment. His old house is for the homeless now, and teens that need a place to misbehave. How many bad elvish poems have been written, how many virginities have been lost, how many pottied plants have been smoked, how many darts have been thrown by others in this derelict building is a mystery for the ages. As Walace walks away from it, without his drink of water, without even a vision of his wife, he thinks that if his cell phone were operating, he would call the fire department and ask them to burn down this fire trap.

But as he walks along like his homeless half-elf hero, he thinks up the hopeful tale that will make a happy ending for Werther's unlucky parents. He will tell the story of the Shade King, who finds Tithon in his cave, wasted to nothing but some dust and a voice, a voice that the Shad King frees from his prison of a frail body by a magic fire that burns clean the soul of the sylph. Tithon thanks the Shade King, and asks whether he has seen Syd.

The Shade King will answer, "She cannot come back to you,

sylph, for she has been transformed into a nightingale. She is no longer called Syd, but Syzygy. She does not remember her old name. She does not remember her life as an elf. She will not remember you, unless you teach her to love you again. Sing to her, sylph, for a nightingale is always looking for the song of her mate. Since you are a gypsy, I command that you search all of Summerheim, and when you find her, you too shall be remade into a nightingale, and when you are reunited, your son may finally lay his sorrows to rest, and the three of you shall be made three stars, aligned, guide stars for all of Summerheim."

Walace likes this. He likes it so much, he dreams that it might be true for him, and Laura-Lynn, and their love child; his book, *The Sorrow of the Elves.*

SEVEN

Always Darkest Before the Dawn

The sulfurous glow of streetlamps plot to keep Walace's face lit like the sun, for he is our hero. When did it get dark again? Walace has not noticed, because he has been walking for hours, and he is high, and he has not slept in two days, and his brain is tired. Don't tell anybody, but Walace secretly loves to make his brain tired, because it makes him see things that are not there, or see things that are there, but see them completely wrong. The real reason he didn't notice that it is night again is because he stood outside the public garden plots staring at somebody's tomato plants for three hours, thinking that he was actually seeing elves, lined in rows, readying their jackrabbits for battle. Part of him knew—part of him always knows—that this is a figment of his tired brain, but part of him likes to run with the figment. He is so creative when his brain is this tired. If he could only remember how to spell words.

Walace likes the night. Bright lights always hurt his dilated eyes, and he has never seen or heard anything too scary in his visions (he hears sounds, too, that are not there). Cal does all the time. It is why he took apart Walace's computer.

Walace likes the night because he can take off this long-sleeved shirt and his sport coat now, which have been so hot. The bruises cannot be seen so well in the dark, the little eggplant stains surrounded by yellow stains, sunspots on the sun king. Still, when he walks under neon signs now and then, unhealed sores, like battle scars, look like chains of lakes seen from an airplane window in a setting sun, gleaming in the shine. "It is the old wound, my king," Walace says out loud, thinking of how he will write about the meeting between the Elf King and his long-lost best friend, Werther, their friendship torn apart by the choices of Lancelotte, which will be the next-to-last chapter of *The Sorrow of the Elves.*

Two teenaged boys on bikes, intending to tease Walace, hear him talking to himself and steer their bikes the other way without even discussing the matter.

It is nice to feel an evening breeze on his bare skin, even nicer when he is high. A ladybug lands on Walace. He knows because its hard red shell with black spots also shines in the streetlamps. "Ladybug, ladybug, fly away home," he chants. "Your house is on fire, your children will burn." Such a dark little rhyme! But all the good ones have a little darkness to them, so that the sun in them burns brighter.

He stops in the middle of the road

to look at the ladybug, because he was told as a child to recite the rhyme and make a wish and blow on the ladybug to make it fly away home and grant your wish. A car swerves by him while he is wishing. It may be that he wishes not to be hit by a car, which is why it does not, but who can be sure about wishes? When he blows on the ladybug, however, it does not fly away to her flaming house. It bites him. Hard.

This is not a ladybug. This is one of those phony ladybugs that have been brought to America from some other place in bundles of firewood that kill off all the good ladybugs and bite children and do not grant wishes. There is, in fact, a corner room of his house that has been locked up because these mean alien fake ladybugs have nested in the ceiling tiles, and while he has not yet called the exterminators, this is a job for professionals. Where are the gentle ladybugs of yesteryear?

He slaps the fake ladybug and at once regrets it. He knows that killing a ladybug is bad luck, even a phony ladybug. "Lady" is a four-letter word. Perhaps this ladybug had come from his own home, to deliver a message? Villains have been known to save themselves in the final chapter.

He looks toward Summerheim. Has he been wandering all night? For there is the dawn, a pink glow over the woods in front of his home. But his house is west of town, and the sun rises in the east! That's not the dawn—that's Summerheim!

And Walace Weiss, to the sound of a loud trumpet reserved for heroes fighting their last battle, begins to run. Only he can save Summerheim.

EIGHT

Slaying the Dragon

I know what you are thinking. All the signs have led us to this moment, when the drug attic has exploded, and a fire has destroyed our hero's home and friend and anything that exists of the manuscript, *The Sorrow of the Elves*. Even Walace Weiss thinks this. He is running up the street as quick as a turkey can run, those quick short legs under that wide-hipped body rushing like a sandpiper outrunning a small wave. A small wave is a tidal wave to an elf.

But there is no fire. That was not Summerheim. That was the dawn. Our hero's tragic flaw is his bad sense of direction. In fact, the house is as dark as a tomb. The gates, with their sad iron elvish curlicues, are ajar, so that just any riffraff can walk right in.

But the riffraff was already there, and already gone.

Walace steps in the hallway, careful not to stumble on any furniture in the dark. But there is nothing left to stumble upon. In the kitchen, he turns on the overhead stove light, the same stove we saw at the beginning of our hero's journey.

There is a note on the kitchen counter. The note is oddly well written. "You think you are so smart.

Well look here, Professor Smarty-Pants. I cleaned you out."

What are you, thinks Walace, the narrator? Narrators are always pointing out the obvious.

Cal writes, "Don't try to call the police, because I already told them about you." It is signed by Cal with a big C turned into a hammer and a sickle, as if he were a commie rebel come to end the old world and start a new one. That is what villains do in the old stories. Take the world that is not theirs and make it their own.

Walace Weiss knows this. He knows that this crook, this betrayer, this Cal, will be his greatest enemy ever. He is not sure he can battle such an enemy. Alone. He wishes that the house were burned to the ground. Then he could believe that it was only an accident. Then he would not feel as empty as Summerheim.

Oh, no. Not Cal. Walace does not want Cal to be the villain. He loves Cal too much. It would be like fighting his own best friend, his own brother. And now, what will he do without his sidekick? What will he do without his Caliban, his Robin Hood, his Loki, his Green Knight, his Grinch?

"The heart dilates," he says to himself, though it is not doing anything of the sort. There isn't even a phone to call the police, who have been told about him. He wanders from room to room trying to recall what was in each of them, but now that they are empty, he is stumped. What is missing in my life? he thinks. I have not told you about so many things he had, the mother and father and two brothers and a sister—a twin sister, in fact, which did not fit into the story, though it fits into a story. There is another story, too, where there were children, and prizes, and friends. These do not belong to this story, either, but they fit into a story.

For now, there is nothing, not even the fuel for his darts, for Cal has taken that, too. Walace Weiss falls on a bed, when he finally finds one in his great scuttled ship of a house. He fights sleep, and sounds he thinks he hears but are not there, and fires he thinks he sees down the hall. He fights the

fact that Cal is not his friend. H
fights these things, and loses.

NINE

Our Hero at Rest

Is this the end for our hero? But Walace Weiss is more than a hero. He is all the characters he has ever dreamed or stolen. Aren't we all? He must only choose which character inside him will win the fight.

He sleeps, and he dreams. He dreams of finding Cal and telling stories and getting back to the way things were. He is alone in his dreaming, but we all are, so do not think for a moment that Walace is alone because he does not love, because Walace loves more

than any of us. He especially loves the people and things that are gone, that can never come back. He loves Uncle Davis, he loves Laura-Lynn, all the girls, all the friends, the stories, all of Summerheim, his home and homeland. He even loves Cal. It is just that he loves one other thing more than all those things—he loves it with wild endless searching selfless selfishness, and it is not clear whether he loves it more than he loves himself. He is on a quest to find out.

In the morning, I assure you, Walace will be all right. He will still be high for a few more days, because it stays inside him for a long time. Cal's potion swirls around in his blood like the snow in snow globes. He will feel strong like an ox and weak like a kitten in the same minute. Then he will be tired for many days, and he will hate that. But now Cal is gone. Now the potion is gone. Now the magic is gone. The terrible smell of his meth lab is gone. His furniture is gone, too. With so much gone, he will try his hardest to leave his truest love. The hardest battle is coming, but he will want to fight. He wants to go on this quest. He has for many years. He will need help. He will need help from those who love him.

His quest is endless, exhausting, and yes, full of sorrow. In his dream, on the bed in the empty house, just there, at the quiet limit of the world, he can hear the nightingale Syzygy, singing her sad song without words. And is that not her weary mate, the gypsy sylph Tithon, himself shrunk to nothing but a voice over the windswept meadows of Summerheim, reunited at last with his warrior wife? And there is Werther, crossing the meadow with a golden cage held up to the sun, the fixed and never-ending sun of Summerheim!

You don't believe in his dream? You do not believe that all this healing can happen? Then do the next best thing to believing: fantasize. There are a hundred roads from this bed, and Walace Weiss must take one of them. He needs a song to sing on his journey in the morning. Sing to him. Sing for him. Let us sing a hymn full of

rhythm to the myth of the gypsy sylph
who dreams there are words without
vowels!